RAMI'S SNOW DAY

by
Candace Rowe

This edition first published in 2022
by Lawley Publishing,
a division of Lawley Enterprises LLC

Lawley Publishing
70 S. Val Vista Dr. #A3 #188
Gilbert, AZ 85296
www.LawleyPublishing.com

Text Copyright © 2022 Candace Rowe
Illustration Copyright © 2022 by Candace Rowe
All Rights Reserved

Hardcover ISBN 978-1-956357-77-6
Paperback ISBN 978-1-956357-79-0
Library of Congress Control Number: 2022934139

For Rami Laith Al-Jamal Judkins - I love being your Pink.

The air was cold, and the sky was gray through frost-painted pictures on the windowpane.

Mom scooped up Rami with a kissing sound,

then wrapped,

wrapped,

wrapped

Rami's scarf around.

Mittens, boots, and hat on head,
she had a big surprise, she said!
Bundled now, both Mom and him,
they opened up the door, and the wind rushed in!

It swirled and twirled and stung his nose,

and whooshed,

whooshed,

whooshed

flurries to-and-fro.

Rami stomped on crunchy ground
and left his footprints all around.
Both Mom and Rami clapped and danced
and caught floaty snowflakes
in their mittened hands.

Then waved Dad with a sled in tow.
They tugged, tugged, tugged—slipped and slid on snow.

Way up the hill to the tippy top,
Dad climbed on, and up Rami hopped!
With a push from Mom, the sled took off.
Then fast, faster, fastest they flew aloft.
Down so fast they flew, and then
they hopped off the sled and climbed the hill again!

Toes and nose were red and cold,
so back to the house, the family strolled.

Rami rode on Dad's warm back.

He bounced,

bounced,

bounced

on a piggyback.

Through the yard and up the stairs,
dripping boots by the fire, soggy coats on chairs.

Snow fell softly in the night
as Rami slept snuggled oh so tight.

Want more insightful, empowering, fun children's books?
Want activities and links to go along with the story?
Visit us at www.lawleypublishing.com

For updates and info on New Releases follow us at

  lawleypublishing @kidsbookswithheart

CPSIA information can be obtained
at www.ICGtesting.com
Printed in the USA
BVHW061915201022
649913BV00002B/4